SIX FRIENDS ONE DISGUISED

AARINI ARZARE

Made with ♥ on the Notion Press Platform
www.notionpress.com

To my parents, brother, grandparents, teachers, and friends.

Contents

Foreword

As I sit down to write this foreword, I feel a mix excitment and nervousness. It's not everyday that a student gets to introduce their very first book to the world, but here I am, writing down these words.

I've always like to write mysteries, although, usually my stories are google ideas and all I do is to elaborate the main plot. But this one is my own idea. I've always felt drawn towards mysteries and thrillers. Whenever I read mysteries or thrillers, I feel like reading even more. It is this fascination for thriller, that has ultimately led me to write 'Six Friends One Disguised'.

The journey of writing this book has become a short adventure for me. I remeber all the late nights I used to sit till twelve or one to complete this book. I still remeber those nights, when I hunched over my laptop to write this. I've discovered different characters of this story, of whom some of them are inspired by my friends.

In 'Six Friends One Disguised', readers will find themselves immeresed in a world were there is nothing like it seems it is. Set against the backdrop of an abandoned mansion in Italy, where these six friends go for an adventure and a change of atmosphere. But nothing is the way it seems it is.

To those who are about to embark on this journey with me, I extend my deepest gratitude. Your curiosity and support mean more to me than words can express. I hope that "Six Friends One Disguised" will captivate and enthrall you, and that you'll join me in unraveling the secrets hidden within its pages.

With Warmest Regards,

Aarini

Acknowledgements

I would like to express my heartfelt gratitude to everyone who contributed to the creation of this book. Writing it has been an incredible journey, and I am deeply thankful for the support and encouragement I received along the way.

First and foremost, I want to thank my mother and father for believing in me and their endless patience during the hours I spent writing this. Your love and encouragement supported me through the highs and lows of the writing process.

I am also indebted to my friends like Idika, Saanvi and Smriti for their constant encouragment and entusiasm of my work.

To my teachers, Ms. Ankana Kundu and Ms. Sunita Abraham, who supported me in every single step I took to write this book. I dedicate this book to Ms. Rekha Tiwari, who supported me and held my hand in every step I took.

Lastly, but certainly not least, I want to express my deepest gratitude to the readers. Your support and enthusiasm for my work mean more to me than words can express. It is a privilege to share this story with you, and I hope it brings you as much joy as it has brought me.

Thank You,

Aarini

Prologue

From the start, people had said that she had a lack of empathy. She had very few friends when she was a child.

One of her only friends had died in a car accident seven years ago and everybody except her was crying on that day, but she just tilted her head at her bleeding friend and laughed. It was the day her parents had left her.

People called her a psychopath. She used to laugh at people's pain. People said that she showed little concern for the feelings or well-being of those around her.

Although she was supposed to cry on the day her parents left her on the streets, she laughed and laughed at her fate, building a small shelter near a big house. A family took her in but was gone missing in a few days.

Since then, no one entered that big mansion, for fear of going missing. She had been only ten when this happened, but after seven years, she was still living in that same big mansion, all alone.

As she returned home, an orphan, who had been lying to her friends about her true personality.

She carried the weight of her lies. Pretending to be someone had now drained her, she wanted to show them her true self, but they would freak out and they would leave her, and she would be lost and alone again.

Boredom crept in, leaving her unsure of what to do next. Exhaustion weighed heavily on her from pretending for so long. It was hard to keep up the act.

Every moment felt like a struggle, each interaction a reminder of her deception. Living a lie was taking its toll. Her patience levels were going down.

Then, an idea popped up in her mind, kidnapping...

CHAPTER ONE

HOMEWORK

Luna's head was resting lightly on the car's window with her nose sticking to it. She was having a nap on her way to school. Luna was a short, healthy girl with long silky hair till her waist. Her hair was a light shade of brown. She had almond eyes with long eyelashes. Her skin was a shade of walnut and she always had perfect nails which were not too long nor too short. Her hobbies included playing guitar and piano, she also absolutely loved playing basketball. Luna could get into a fight or jump into an argument whenever needed, or at places, not needed.

The car jerked and Luna woke up with a start. She didn't know how time flew past by so quick. The last time her eyes were open was just a few minutes ago, if she remembered it correctly.

She looked at herself in the rearview mirror and straightened out her hair which were popping out of her headband. While she was busy setting her hair, she heard someone shout her name. She looked back to find Lily running towards her. Luna had met her on the first day of high school and they became best friends almost immediately.

Lily joined the school with her this year.

Luna had stopped dead in her tracks and shrunk herself to the smallest size. Time seemed to slow down as Lily came rushing towards her.

Lily gave Luna a big bear hug which seemed to break her ribcage. After some centuries (or what had seemed like centuries), she held Luna's hand and dragged her towards the school.

She finally stopped dragging Luna and looked at her. She was only a bit taller than her.

'Hey, Penelope was searching for you. She said she had messaged you something on WhatsApp yesterday but you didn't reply.'- said Lily.

'Oh no,'- said Luna. 'Where is she?'- she asks hurriedly.

Lily pointed towards a bench where a girl was sitting. Luna ran towards Penelope and said 'I am really sorry that I couldn't send you yesterday's English work.'- she said, and she meant it.

'It's okay, but can you lend me your English notebook?'- said Penelope kindly. Without wasting a minute, she opened her bag, took out her English notebook and gave it to Penelope.

Penelope was a tall, skinny girl with a bob cut, complete moon spectacles, sky-blue eyes, fair skin and with long fingers. She was a kind, adventure loving girl who always liked exploring new places and sites. She loved talking and studying about dinosaurs. She didn't talk much. Although she was a kind-hearted person, everybody expected her to have many friends. But she had very less friends as she was the definition of introvert.

Once she handed the book to Penelope, she left to talk with Lily.

'Where are the others?'- Luna asked Lily. Lily didn't answer but was looking behind her and Luna got her answer.

She looked back and saw three guys walking towards them. 'Here are the others'- she muttered under her breath, rolled her eyes and crossed

her arms.

Oliver, James and Jacob were walking towards them.

'Hi Ms. Perfect,'- Oliver said to Luna mischievously. 'Not again.'- said Luna and gave a big sigh.

'And Ms. Bear hug', he said to Lily with a slight smug on his face and completely ignored Luna's muttering.

'Of course, how can we miss Ms. Studious.'- he said and looked at Penelope. 'Mr. Smelly and Mr. Dirty Socks'- he said to James and Jacob.

'The best acting I have ever seen of the big, bad bully Edith'- said Jacob with absolute sarcasm in his voice and James nodded his head in agreement.

Oliver was a tall, healthy boy with extremely long hair that covered his eyebrows and one could tie a pony from it. Although his hair looked like a bird's nest, it suited him. He had doe eyes with short eyelashes and olive-green eyes. He had a dimple on his right cheek and had thin lips. He loved to draw and paint in his free time and was a by-heart fan of marvel. His hobbies included, teasing, annoying and pulling pranks on Penelope, Luna, and Lily. He was the heart of the group.

James was a thin and sporty boy. He had short and bushy hair. His glasses covered his dark brown eyes. He had thin lips and big eyelashes. James never liked to talk about his family, and nobody ever tried to persuade him. He also loved watching comedy movies and read books in his free time. His hobbies included listening to Jacob and Oliver, and to follow them blindly.

Jacob was a thin and tall boy; in fact, he was the tallest in the gang, only an inch higher than Oliver, although Oliver considered him his height. He loved playing football and was considerable at basketball. He was the best striker in the school and also had been selected for the school football team. He had an army cut and nobody could ever name single day he was late for school. He was also excellent in studies. He had beautiful grey eyes and big eyelashes. His skin was the shade of almond. His hobbies included playing football and teaming up with Oliver to pull pranks.

They were just talking and then arguing and then back to normal. This was their daily routine. They were just going to start a debate on who was more annoying but just then the bell rang and they all hurried off to their classrooms (All of them were in the same class).

Penelope closed her books and was now walking towards Luna to return her English notebook. She was about to catch up with Luna but that's when Oliver caught up with her and said, 'Hey, did Luna inform you about the math homework which we had to compete by today. Yeah, and also today is the last day of submission.' And then scurried off to join the talk with James and Jacob.

Penelope did not want to believe Oliver but, what if he was right and was not just fooling around?

She tapped Luna's shoulder lightly and handed over the book. Luna was just about to say, 'thank you'.

But before she could say anything, Penelope shouted, 'Why didn't you tell me there was math homework? I asked you about a million times, if there was something else you forgot to tell me!'

That came out louder than she had expected. She slammed the book so hard in Luna's hand that it turned a slight shade of pink.

'Ouch, that hurts Penelope! Are you out of your mind?!'- said Luna, her temper rising.

Penelope opened her mouth to argue, when Luna said, 'Oh please Penelope, can you stop for a minute and not spoil my mood in the morning', her voice so loud that it caused several people to look around to see what was happening.

Color was rising to Penelope's face. Luna clenched her fist and was about to punch Penelope when Lily put her hand on Luna's shoulder and muttered into her ear, 'Luna don't, people are watching.'

She looked around and saw that people were filming them. She turned to see Penelope but she was now lost in the crowd.

Luna, now pushed people aside and entered the class. To her utter dismay, Penelope was going to sit right behind her.

'Why is she sitting behind me, why me?'- thought Luna. As though Penelope had read her mind, she said 'I couldn't find any other place to sit.'

Ignoring her, Luna and Lily sat together in front of Penelope. 'Come on Luna, she is such a good friend of yours. Just make it up with her. You are spoiling both yours and her mood.'- said Lily, trying to comfort her.

Just when Luna opened her mouth to argue, Mr. Rupert entered their class (He was their math teacher). Everyone greeted him and settled down.

When the muttering and talking had died out, Mr. Rupert said, 'Before we start Chapter-7, I would like your math notebooks and-, yes Ms. Stirling,'- he said and pointed towards Penelope.

The whole class turned around to see Penelope. She hesitated for a while before speaking and then spoke loud and clear, 'Mr. Rupert, I am really sorry I couldn't complete my math homework. I didn't know about it, I wasn't informed. I am really, really sorry. I will complete it by tomorrow, just give me a chance.'- she said pleadingly.

'What homework are you talking about Ms. Stirling, I don't understand.'- he asked. 'The homework which you gave yesterday.'- She said in a-matter-of-fact voice. 'I clearly remember that I gave no homework yesterday.'- he said flatly.

Penelope opened her mouth to argue but Mr. Rupert said 'I gave no homework yesterday; you have been made a fool of and end of the conversation. I wish to hear no more. Kindly be seated.'- he said sternly.

The whole class burst into laughter and Penelope sat down, embarrassed.

Although Luna's fight with Penelope, she felt bad for her.

She looked at the whole class laughing and her eyes fell on Oliver, she saw him sniggering.

The moment she saw him, she knew something was wrong, she knew exactly what was wrong. She raised her hand and waited for Mr. Rupert to see her raised hand. Mr. Rupert got hold of the class and gestured Luna to stand up.

'Yes Ms. Lockwood, what may be your question?'- said Mr. Rupert plainly.

'Sir, I saw Oliver talking to Penelope in the morning.'- said Luna. 'So?'- asked Mr. Rupert, a bit annoyed now. 'What I am trying to say is that,'- She paused and continued, now that she was aware that Oliver was watching her, along with the rest of the class.

'We all know that Oliver is very mischievous and will stop at nothing to trouble someone. So, I believe that Oliver was the one who told Penelope about the homework, when there was none.'- she ended and sat down.

'Is it true Ms. Stirling?'- asked Mr. Rupert.

Penelope simply nodded.

'Mr. Holloway, I would like you to stop for some time and follow me in the staffroom after the class ends, is that clear Mr. Holloway? I would like to have a little chat with you.'- said Mr. Rupert sternly.

Oliver gave Luna a I'll-deal-with-you-later-look and apologized to Mr. Rupert.

'This is the last time I want to hear this. If I hear something like this again, I will have to call your parents and issue a warning letter.'- said Mr. Rupert severely.

With this, the bell rang and the class ended. Oliver gave the same scornful look to Luna and didn't look at her for the whole day.

The classes continued and ended very quickly that day.

Nothing else happened for the rest of the day.

CHAPTER TWO

THE PLAN

It was the last period that had ended now and Penelope came running towards Luna and Lily. She caught her breath and said 'I... I... am really... sorry about what happened in the morning. I lost control. I didn't mean to hurt you, and... thank you for having my back.' 'It's okay. I am sorry as well.'- said Luna. 'I am happy that you guys made it up.'- said Lily, bursting with happiness.

'Guys,'- said Penelope, 'I think we should leave.'- she said, the smile had faded from her face. 'Why,'- asked Lily absent mindedly. 'Oliver and the others are coming.'- said Luna. 'I think we should run.'- said Penelope. 'Yeah right.'- said Lily, they ran and hid behind a car. 'Luna, I think- Luna, where are you?!'- said Lily, realizing that Luna was not behind the car. 'Oh no.'- said Penelope. 'She is still there; we have to go. Now.' They both ran towards Luna and found her talking casually with Oliver, James and Jacob. 'Hey, see, Lily and Penelope are here too.'- said Jacob, spotting them. 'Come on, join us.'- said James enthusiastically. Realizing that there was nothing wrong, Lily and Penelope joined James, Jacob and Oliver.

'What did we miss?'- asked Lily excitedly. 'As it is the last day of school,'- started James. 'We were planning to go somewhere with you guys.'- ended Jacob. 'No, the plan was for a sleepover, wasn't it Oliver?'- interrogated James. Oliver shrugged his shoulders as though he didn't want to take a part in the argument. Jacob and James both started to talk at the same time and nobody was able to understand what they were saying when both of them suddenly said 'Okay then, done.' 'We are going to go somewhere out.'- said James. Lily looked at Jacob and he seemed completely fine with it.

There was a moment of silence that was not awkward. It was the silence that agreed to the idea of going out. The silence after that was awkward. Oliver broke the silence and said 'So, where are we going to go?' 'A movie?'- suggested James. 'Horror films, it'll be wonderful!'- said Lily enthusiastically.

'No, I am scared of ghosts. A comedy movie maybe?'- suggested Penelope. 'No. never. Comedy films make me fall asleep.'- said Luna.

'I have one suggestion that you all will like.'- said Jacob. This made everyone look at him. 'Let's not watch a movie, let's go on a trek or something like that.'- said Jacob.

'Just because you like to play football and you are a sporty person, that doesn't mean that we all like to get tanned and get all sweaty in the hot sun.'- said Lily. 'So, what should we do then?'- said Jacob, sounding a bit annoyed. 'Go sneak out at night and go kill someone?'- he said with sarcasm. 'Nice idea.'- said Oliver, without understanding the hint of sarcasm in his voice. This made everyone look at him. 'What?'- he said, confused.

All of them ignored him and Lily was the one who spoke up, 'I think we can go for an adventure tonight, or go visit the graveyard near Luna's house, or we could go in the park beside James's house, in the night, or could play video games at Jacob's house or... any suggestions?' 'I think we should go on a spooky adventure in an abandoned place and don't you worry Penelope, we all will be there with you.'- said Jacob. 'Yeah.'- said Luna.

'Okay, so is it decided that we will be going to some abandoned place tonight? Is everyone okay with that? If not, I don't care. I will not miss out on all the fun because of you. If everyone's coming, say yes or yep or whatever, or just make a gesture which agrees if you are coming.'- said Oliver, saying something sensible for the first time.

'Yep'

'Yeah'

'Yes'

'Of course,'

'I'm so ready'

'If everyone's okay with it, why don't we find any places which we will be visiting.'- said Oliver, saying something sensible for the second time in a day.

'Does anyone have any ideas about any place we should visit, that are haunted, or at least the places that are said to be haunted.'- said James.

'I think we should-, hey Penelope, I think we crossed your house.'- said Jacob. 'I think your house was in the previous lane.'- said Luna. 'I think your house is the next one.'- said Lily. 'No, we crossed my house, it was in the previous lane.'- said Penelope. 'Okay then, see you later.'- said Oliver. 'Hey Luna, isn't your house adjacent to hers?'- said Lily. 'Yeah, I'll leave.'- said Luna. 'Bye.'- all of them said in unison.

Luna and Penelope just started to walk when Oliver called out 'I will call you in the evening at four, don't hang up.' 'I will not hang up.'- said Luna and started to walk back home.

Everyone was now home and were having an afternoon nap, except Jacob, who was searching for 'haunted places to visit' on the net.

Penelope got a call from Oliver and of course, she picked it up. Then came Jacob, then came Luna, then James and Lily. 'So, Jacob, did you find any places that we could go to?'- asked Oliver.

'Before we start to discuss anything, I have got a problem.'- said Penelope. 'Will our parents allow us to go?' This seemed to get everyone's attention. 'My parents allowed me to go.'- said James. 'I will have to find some excuse to go.'- said Penelope. 'My parents don't even care what I do, so... I am coming.'- said Oliver. 'I will have to sneak out.'- said Luna. 'Same for me.'- said Lily. 'But it won't be long before your parents find out you are not home.'- said Jacob.

'You are filthy rich dude, you have your own car, your parents don't even care.'- said Oliver to Jacob. 'That's right, and I will come to pick you guys up from your houses'- said Jacob.

'Can we decide the location which we will be going to?'- asked Lily. 'Yeah'- said James.

'Okay, so this house or rather say mansion, is where we will be going to. I will read out the information about it that is available on google. Here it goes- Located near Lake Como, Italy, the "House of Witches" dates back to 1854-1857, when it was built as a summer house for Count Felix De Vecchi. The family was only able to spend a few years there, as their lives were mired in tragedy right after it was built. First, the architect died a year after construction. Then in 1862, Count De Vecchi came home to discover his wife murdered and his daughter missing. When he could not find her after a year of searching, he died by suicide.

His brother then moved into the home and his family continued to live there until WWII. It's been vacant since the 1960s, and an avalanche in 2002 wiped out all the houses in the area... except this one.

'Spooky'- said Oliver.

'Can't we look for some other places?'- asked Penelope. 'Are you scared?'- asked James teasingly. 'No, it's not that.'- she said.

'Penelope's right, I think we should look for some other place.'- said Luna. 'Why, are you too scared to go?'- asked Oliver 'That place is located in Italy.'- said Penelope. 'Can't we find something closer?' asked Luna. 'There would be no internet towers around. We won't be able to contact help, even if we tried to.'- said Lily. 'And there won't be any charging points. What if the batteries from our phone died out?'- added Penelope.

'Oh, please guys, this is such a good place, why are you disagreeing.'- said James. 'Yes, James is right, we will not miss the fun because of three scaredy cats.'- said Oliver and then sniggered.

'We, are going and we don't care if you come or not.'- said Jacob. 'We will not miss out on the fun because of you.'- said James. 'We are leaving tomorrow morning.'- said James. 'It's up to you if you want to come or not.'- said Oliver.

'Fine, I will come.'- Luna. 'Me too.'- said Lily. 'Yeah, okay.'- said Penelope. 'Yayyy, finally the scaredy cats agreed to come.'- said Oliver teasingly.

'Oh, yes, just saying that we will be going from car and it will be a one and a half days' drive.'- said Jacob.

'I'm carsick.'- said Luna.

CHAPTER THREE

THE DRIVE FINALLY STARTS

'Hey, Oliver, I'm outside your house, come quick.'- said Jacob on the phone. 'Yep, coming.'- said Oliver from the other side of the phone. 'Hi, good morning, Ms. Perfect. Jacob is waiting outside your house, and just if you were wondering, this is Oliver speaking from Jacob's phone.'- said Oliver, with Jacob in the car.

'Coming.'- said Penelope.

'Good morning, dear passenger, the weather today is a bit gloomy, so buckle up your seatbelt as we are going to fly to Italy.'- said Jacob.

'Firstly, how much time did you spend on preparing this,'- said Luna. 'Secondly, the best pilot I have ever seen.'- she said with the absolute sarcasm in her voice.

'Hi, Mr. Dirty socks, kindly come down.'- said Oliver. 'Of, course, it's been a pleasure serving you Donkey Holloway.'- said James loyally.

'Come on quick, we need to leave, what are you doing Lily!'- said Luna, annoyed, after waiting for fifteen minutes outside Lily's house.

'Just a second.'- said Lily impatiently from the other side of the phone. After what seemed like some more fifteen minutes, Lily came rushing out of the front door. 'OMG Lily, what took you saw long?'- said Luna, annoyed. Ignoring Luna's annoyed face, Lily leapt in for a hug.

Narrowly missing Lily's big bear hug, Luna almost tripped.

When Lily finally got inside the car, James said 'What took you so long?' Before Lily could answer, Jacob spoke up 'We had a plan to leave by 7:45.' 'Yeah, and its already 8:00.'- said Oliver. 'I'm really sorry guys, I was so excited to go that I didn't sleep all night. I was reading a book and I fell asleep at six. When you guys called, I hadn't even brushed or taken a bath, what's more is that I forgot to pack my suitcase.'- said Lily.

'Wonderful.'- Penelope muttered to herself. 'We all were excited, but we were sensible enough to not stay awake all night.'- said Luna. Lily opened her mouth to argue but James stopped him by saying- 'Let's not argue, all right.' By saying this, nobody spoke for a while.

'Jacob, can you stop the car for a while and park it in a corner?'- asked Luna. 'Why.'- asked Oliver. 'Didn't I tell you, I'm carsick.'- said Luna. 'Oh yeah.'- said Jacob. 'Just a minute, and... yeah, you can get down here.'- he said.

Luna swiftly got out of the car and said, 'Guys, please don't look at me.', after she saw all the five pair of eyes looking at her. After few disgusting vomiting sounds, Luna got back in the car.

'Anyone here has a mouth freshener?'- asked Luna hopefully. 'Here you go,' said James. 'Thanks.'- she said and ate one of the mouth fresheners.

After what seemed like an hour of silence, Lily broke the it and said 'Hey guys, does anyone have anything to eat?

The thing is that- oh wait, did anyone bring food, because we will be needing food if we don't want to die out of hunger.'

'I brought food, don't know about anyone else.'- said James. 'Yeah, even I brought food.'- said Penelope. 'Even I brought food. Actually, I brought so much food that it would be enough for ten heavy eaters to survive for a week.'- said Jacob. 'Oohhh, what all did you bring?'- asked Lily, taking interest in the topic.

'Nothing much', - said Jacob. 'I brought junk food and fruits. In fruits I brought- a dozens of bananas, two watermelons, three apples, three or four oranges, don't remember precisely, two pears, two pineapples, two blueberries and one more fruit, don't remember. For junk food, I brought- one cheesecake of five hundred grams, seven hundred fifty grams of chocolate biscuits, a hundred grams of chocolate biscuits with chocolate chips, and... yes, four bars of dairy milk and eight bars of five-star chocolates.'- he said.

Before anyone could say anything, he said, 'Yeah, and I also brought two boxes of donuts with nine donuts in each box.' When nobody seemed to ask any questions or show any interests in the topic, Jacob turned back and saw that everyone (except Oliver, who was sitting in the front seat beside him) was playing hangman. 'Hey guys,'- said Jacob and everyone hurriedly looked up and closed the book which was lying in Luna's lap.

On this final note, he looked back front and focused fully on his driving. It was a bit of a shock that a seventeen-year-old was driving a car, that too so swiftly and expertly. He was also looking back several times and talking to the group sitting behind. He himself was surprised that he didn't crash the car while looking behind and talking, and it was not as if he was trying to show off or something.

After what seemed like fifteen minutes, James said, 'Uhm... guys, let's take a break here, it's such a good weather outside, and the scenery here is so good. It's so peaceful.'

Jacob stopped the car and everyone stepped outside the it. Penelope yawned and stretched herself. 'It feels so good to be here. It's calming.'- she said.

'We've officially covered seven hours of our journey.'- said Jacob and there was a lot of cheering and whooping at this line.

'Hey guys, lets sit here.'- said James. 'There?!'- exclaimed Penelope. James nodded in agreement. 'It's a mountain cliff dude.'- said Lily. 'Do you want us to die!'- said Penelope. 'Come on Penelope, enjoy. You never know if we can ever see this scene ever again in our lives.'- said Luna. 'Yes Penelope, what's fun without a little danger. That feeling is always wonderful when your heartbeat increases and you know its dangerous but you do it anyways.'- said Jacob soothingly.

They all sat down at the edge with their feet dangling from the edge. 'Hey, guys, I just wrote something about this place and this scene. I want you to hear it out before I put it on Insta.'- said Jacob.

'Yeah sure, let's hear it out.'- said James.

Jacob took a deep breath and read out- 'Perched on the edge of a rugged mountain cliff, me, along with my friends- Oliver, James, Penelope, Luna and Lily, find ourselves amidst breathtaking views and exhilarating heights. Our legs dangling over the edge of the cliff, we all share a moment of pure bliss.

Luna and James sit the closest to the precipice, with their legs swinging freely in the open air, while the others gather around them, each finding their own spot on the rocky outcrop (except Penelope, who, of course is a bit afraid of heights).

Luna leans back against the solid rock, arms outstretched as if embracing the vast expanse of sky above and

Oliver balances precariously on a nearby boulder, a mischievous grin on his face as he playfully teases his companions.

In the distance, the sun casts a warm evening glow over the rolling mountains and valleys below, painting the landscape in one last hue of orange and gold. A gentle breeze sweeps through the air, carrying the scent of pine and the distant sound of birdsong. Together, we laugh and share stories, our voices mingling with the whispers of the wind and the distant rumble of cascading waterfalls. In this moment, high above the world, we all find a sense of freedom and connection that binds us together as friends forever.'- ended Jacob.

'How was it?'- he asked.

'Beautiful.'- said Penelope. 'Amazing dude.'- said James, patting him on the back. 'I never knew you could write so well.'- said Luna. 'Me too.'- said Lily. 'Oh, I never you could write.'- said Oliver with absolutely no sarcasm in his voice.

'The fact that you wrote it so quickly and beautifully, honestly saying, I had goosebumps in the last two sentences.'- said Luna, ignoring Oliver.

'Thank you, thank you. With this, we end this show and I would request everybody to proceed to the car so that we can leave.'- said Jacob.

'Anyways, does anyone know how to drive?'- he asked.

'I do.'- said James, Luna and Oliver at the same time. 'Actually, I am feeling a bit tired after driving for seven hours, so... umm... can one of you drive, and please be careful. I don't want a single scratch on my car. I hope I can trust you'- said Jacob hopefully and left Oliver, Luna and James to decide how will drive.

'Yeah, okay.'- said Oliver. 'Jacob, till the time we decide who will drive, you can go rest.'- said James.

The moment Jacob sat in the car, he fell asleep, lost in the dreamworld.

'So... who is going to be the first one to drive?'- asked Luna.

'The first one to touch the car will drive first.'- said Oliver and ran off. Luna ran after him and James froze on the spot, processing the information of the current scene. After three or four seconds, James ran to find Oliver already on the driver's seat, with Luna on the seat beside him, looking annoyed. James sat in the back with Jacob, Lily and Penelope.

Lily and James were at the windows while Penelope and Jacob were in the centre. 'Hey,'- Penelope called out to James and Lily, as if trying not to disturb Jacob while he was sleeping.

'Wanna play hangman?'- she asked.

CHAPTER FOUR

WARNING FROM AN OLD MAN

'Hey, James, I want you to describe us six in this open jeep.'- said Penelope. 'Oh, okay, so you want me to describe the scene as a third person or as James.'- he asked. Before Penelope could answer, Lily said, 'Do both.'

'Okay,'- he said and paused for a while to think.

In the meanwhile, Oliver said 'We have completed nine and a half hours.' 'Next half an hour then I am driving.'- said Luna.

'Let's see, what can we do.'- James muttered to himself, ignoring Oliver and Luna. He observed everyone and said, 'I will do the James first – So... umm... according to me, we are six crazy friends, travelling to Italy, just to visit some haunted place named Villa de Vecchi, which is hardly in living condition. It is said that an avalanche in 2002 swept all the houses near and around it, except this one. Anyways, we are completely mad and that's all I could understand about you guys in one year. So.... Now as a third person, right?'- he asked and got a nod from Lily.

He was just about to start speaking when Penelope interrupted and said 'But, there is a twist, you have to say it like Jacob, the way he said it.'

'Okay, I can try...'- he said. 'Let me think.'- he stopped for a minute or two and spoke – 'Six friends ride in the jeep, their laughter carried away by the wind. At the wheel is Oliver, their mischievous driver, with a wide grin on his face as he navigates the rocky terrain with ease. Beside Oliver sits Luna, her hair tousled by the wind as she leans back, taking in the breathtaking scenery and waiting patiently for her chance to drive.

In the back seat, the remaining four friends are packed in snugly. Lily and Penelope sit side by side, their heads thrown back in laughter as they exchange jokes and stories. Across from them, James and Jacob share a quiet moment, lost in conversation as they gaze out at the passing landscape. But amidst all the excitement, one of their friends (Jacob) has succumbed to the gentle sway of the jeep and the soothing hum of the engine. Jacob rests peacefully, his head tilted back against the seat, soft snores escaping his lips as he drifts off into a peaceful and soulful nap.

As the jeep rumbles onward, the friends continue their journey, the bonds of friendship growing stronger with each passing mile.

'Nice.'- said Luna. 'I like it.'- said Penelope. 'I think you and Jacob exchanged your thoughts for a while.'- said Lily.

Oliver stopped the car suddenly and got down. Luna and he exchanged places and Luna got the driver's seat. Just when Luna was about to start driving, Lily said 'Can I sit in the front seat?'- she asked. 'Yeah,'- said Oliver, he was way too tired to argue or say anything else. He got down and Lily took over the front seat beside Luna.

'Hey Luna, can you play the radio?'- asked James. 'Yeah, sure, why not?'- said Luna. Luna played the radio, which overlapped Jacob's soft snores, which were now joined by Oliver. The songs kept playing as night began to fall and the sun began to go down.

***

Penelope could no longer sit next to the door as she was scared of the dark. It was already eight in the night and everyone was feeling hungry, including Jacob and Oliver, who had now woken up. Everyone except Luna (who was busy driving) and Penelope (who was too scared to look outside) were busy finding places where they could stop and eat dinner. After a while Jacob pointed out to a small shop, more like a stall, lined with packed food, although they could not see what food.

Luna stopped the car as she (nor anyone else) could see any more food shops (or any shops at all, to be precise) anywhere nearby. They all got out of the car and proceeded to see what was in the tiny stall.

The moment they got down from the jeep, a strong, cool wind blew which caused all of them to shiver. They all started to walk casually to the stall, all of them hoping to find something warm to eat.

It looked like it was about to snow at any moment. Tall trees were standing around, which made the weather even colder. 'I have a few jackets in the car, shall I bring them?'- asked Jacob when they were almost there. 'Is that even a question.'- asked Luna. Penelope sneezed three times in a row when Luna said it.

'Yeah, we will wait here.'- said Lily and sneezed. 'I will help you out.'- said Oliver, and both of them ran off to get the jackets. The others came and sat down on the stools placed adjacent to the stall.

Luna went to check if someone was there and found an old man sitting inside the shop. 'Yes, how may I help you.'-

asked the old man. 'Can I get six cups of noodles?'- asked Luna. 'Of course, why not?'- the man said sweetly. 'Small, medium, or large.'- he asked. 'Large.'- said Luna and sat down with the others.

The poor, old man seemed to look very friendly.

Oliver and Jacob came running with some jackets in their hands. They both were wearing jackets as well. 'I hope these fit you.'- said Oliver.

'Thank god none of you wore shorts.'- said Jacob. He handed each one a jacket and Penelope was the first one to get it. 'I didn't find another jacket but I found this shawl, will it work?'- he said, handing it over to Luna. Luna nodded simply. 'Have you ordered anything yet?'- asked James. 'Yes, I have ordered six cups of noodles.'-said Luna. 'There it is.'- she said.

The old man was very well bringing six hot cups of noodles. 'Please wait for some time and then open the lid.'- he said sweetly.

'Thank you.'- said Oliver. Everyone stared at him as though he was turning into a zombie the minute. He took the noodles and started distributing the cups to everyone. 'What?'- asked Oliver, realizing that everyone was staring at him.

'You have never said 'thank you' or 'sorry' to anyone.'- said Jacob. 'His voice was so sweet that I couldn't control myself from saying thanks.'- replied Oliver. 'You are right, he does seem friendly.'- agreed Penelope, sneezing once more. They waited in silence for a minute or two and began to eat their noodles. They took a single slurp of their noodles when the old man came with a few logs of wood.

'Children, move aside a bit, will ya', let me put this wood here to keep ya' warm. They all moved their stools to sit in a circle. The old man put the pieces of wood in the middle and hurried off to bring the matchsticks. In a minute or two, the old man brings the matches and lights up the wood. The crackling flames of the roaring fire urge all the friends to move closer to the fire. Although for a short while, these six friends felt cozy and at home. Their hands and body warmed up by the hot ramen.

They finish their food and go up to the old man to give the money. 'How much?'- asked Oliver. 'It's okay children, I don't want to take any money from you.'- said the old man, smiling kindly. Jacob searched for something in his pockets and took out twenty bucks to give to the old man. He took it politely, with no sign of greediness on his face.

All of them start to walk towards the jeep with their hearts full of contentment at the warm service of the old man.

After three seconds or so, the old man called out, 'Where off to?' 'Vila De Vecchi.'- called back James. The comforting toothy grin escaped from the old man's face. 'I am warning you, children, don't go there. Something unfortunate, something unexpected is going to happen. I have seen many people, who go there for adventure... for a visit and they never come back. There is still time, turn around, don't risk your lives.'- he said and closed the lights of his shop once and for all.

'Crazy old man, huh.'- said Luna. 'Of course we won't turn back.'- agreed Oliver. 'I hope we never see that guy again.'- said James. 'Yes, we will never see him again.'- said Penelope. 'What makes you say that?'- asked Jacob. 'Just guessing.'- replied Penelope, shrugging her shoulders.

They all sat inside the car, completely ignoring the old man's warning and continuing the drive. It was already 9 PM and it was now James's turn to drive. Luna sat back and fell asleep almost immediately as the car engine started to chug, drifting into the world of dreams.

Everyone (except Luna, who was of course asleep) was discussing the old man's warning. The old man, who had looked like a comforting and sweet guy at the beginning, now seemed a little weird. The only one who was not taking part in the discussion was Penelope.

While they were talking, Penelope suddenly spoke up, 'Guys,'- this made everyone pay attention to her. 'I think we should turn back.'- she said. For the first time, Penelope's voice was not full of fear. Everyone pondered her advice momentarily, but ultimately dismissed it, collectively deeming her a "scaredy-cat" and "not fond of adventures."

As nightfall descended, a wave of drowsiness enveloped everyone, causing the heavy eyelids to close. James continued to drive as everyone fell asleep. The radio had now been reduced to its minimal volume. The only sound heard was the car's engine sound and the soft snores of Jacob and Oliver.

CHAPTER FIVE

ARRIVING AT VILLA DE VECCHI

The car came to a halt and Jacob woke up with a start. He looked around to see what was happening. He saw James coming towards the back seat and gently put a hand on Jacob's shoulder to wake him up. 'Hey, it's your turn to drive.'- he said softly. Jacob got down to the front seat without arguing and started to drive. It was 2 in the morning when James woke him up. After a minute or two of driving, Jacob began to feel more alert, ready to take the road with renewed energy. He soon started to hear James's snores join the others (Oliver's, as no other person would snore so loudly).

Jacob was driving cautiously and at full speed, with several bumps in the middle, which caused Lily, Penelope, and Oliver to sometimes wake up (but eventually they would go back to sleep). After what seemed three hours, Jacob looked at the time to realize that it was already 5 in the morning. He had the urge to wake up Oliver to drive but decided to let him sleep. Two more hours passed and he couldn't resist the urge to wake Oliver up.

The next moment Oliver was up and brimming with energy, not at all frustrated by the fact that he was being woken up at 7.

Between 7 and 8, everyone was wide awake. They all were filled with energy. The bright morning light of the morning sun illuminated the smiles on their faces. The only person who was not fully charged was Oliver, who was a bit tired after driving. Everyone was shocked to see Oliver tired, as he (and Jacob) was the heart and laughter of the gang. Without him, they would just be a bunch of teenagers hanging around and sharing their sorrows after failing their exams. Jacob, as well was looking a bit moody that day, although, everyone knew that Oliver just needed some rest and he would be back to his crazy self, or, as all of the others called it 'Normal self.'

What people think is crazy, is normal for Oliver.

Luna took over the handle at around twelve, with Oliver back to his 'normal self.' There was no more peace with Jacob and Oliver both wide awake. After some thirty minutes, Luna started to drive, Lily started to feel hungry and they had to stop to eat.

Unlike the last time, this place was somewhat like a restaurant, but with a little less space.

It was a Chinese restaurant, so, there were noodles, Momos, Manchurians, Chow Mein, Spring Rolls, Wonton Soup, etc.

They all ordered different things and decided to share and eat everything. There was no one else in the restaurant except them so their order arrived in hardly twenty minutes. They all delved into the food and gobbled it all up in hardly any time as they didn't have any breakfast in the morning.

The workers of the restaurant must have thought that they hadn't eaten in days.

After they had finished eating the food present on the table, their hunger hadn't died out yet so they ordered some more. The food was again present on the table in twenty minutes and that as well, vanished in a few minutes.

They kept on talking and kept troubling each other (Oliver). They all had a feeling that nothing could go wrong now.

Penelope was strangely very quiet during the talk and she was constantly staring out of the door. Nobody bothered to ask her why as they were busy talking over each other's voices. Lily suggested asking for the bill as none of them wanted to get late to their final destination.

Jacob asked for the bill and paid it in no time. When they were about to leave, the waiter asked- 'Are you children just roaming around or are you heading off somewhere.'

'We are heading to this abandoned house, can't remember the name.'- said James politely. 'All I remember is that it started with a 'V'.'- said Oliver. 'I think it was Villa De Vec- '- said Luna but was interrupted by the waiter.

'STOP! DON'T YOU FOOLISH CHILDREN UTTER THE NAME OF THAT HOUSE IN THIS RESTAURANT! DON'T YOU KNOW WHAT HAPPENS TO THE PERSON WHO SPEAKS THE NAME OF THAT HOUSE AND TO THE PEOPLE RELATED TO HIM!? IT ONLY BRINGS BAD LUCK OR SOMETHING UNFORTUNATE TO THE PERSON!'- on this, the waiter went storming inside the kitchen.

It was almost 2 in the afternoon when they left the restaurant. They all quietly walked back to the car and everyone was processing the information they just heard. They couldn't understand what to do. They didn't ignore the warning of the man. This was the second time that they had heard the same warning. Although there was no need for that waiter to shout like that.

It could not be a solemn coincidence that something unfortunate happened to everyone related to that house. They all were now a bit scared about going to Villa De Vecchi but they decided not to turn around after being so close to their destination. They also decided that they would stick together no matter what happened and would not leave each other's side. In that case, no one would be hurt. They all promised each other that they would not split up. No matter what happens.

Everyone was very quiet during the rest of the drive, pondering about if all these warnings were for their good and if they should turn back to the safety of their house or if it was just some stupid myth, that they had to break.

The drive continued very silently. Luna stopped the car abruptly on the side and James understood it was his turn to drive. It was 7 in the evening when it was James took over the handle.

Luna had taken a nap for about fifteen minutes and then woke up again with a lot of energy. She was looking outside, wondering if something unfortunate would happen. Should she be asking her friends to turn around, to not go to Villa de Vecchi? There were still two hours left. They still hadn't reached Villa de Vecchi yet, there was still time to caution her friends about the danger that might be awaiting them in the shadows of the abandoned mansion. The creepy, old mansion.

At this point, she was sure that no one would listen to her. But she wanted to say it, she could not understand who to say it to. Oliver and Jacob would call her a 'scaredy cat', and James would always support them. Lily, would like to talk about something else and Penelope was just too quiet to speak.

Penelope would understand her, she would listen to her without any questions. Penelope was sitting right beside her.

'Hey Penelope,'- she said. 'Yes?'- Penelope said quietly. 'Can I talk to you for a minute?'- asked Luna. 'Yes, of course, why not.'- said Penelope, closing the book she was drawing in.

'Do you think that we should not be going to that mansion?'- asked Luna. Penelope hesitated but Luna patiently waited for an answer. Penelope nodded and said- 'I suggested this to Oliver but then he disregarded my comment by saying that I was a 'scaredy cat' and was not fond of adventure.'- she said.

Luna gently patted her back, as though trying to comfort her.

'Hey guys, announcement, announcement, we are going to arrive at Villa De Vecchi in one hour.'- said Oliver excitedly

'Do you suggest we should tell him about what we think?'- asked Penelope, her voice barely louder than a whisper. 'They will not listen to us.'- said Luna. 'And neither will they turn around with only one hour left, that too with James driving.'- she said. 'Did you see how excited Oliver was when he said that only an hour was left before we reached Villa de Vecchi.'- said Penelope. 'Yeah, you're right, but it's worth a try.'- said Luna.

'Hey, uhm, Oliver,'- started Penelope quietly. After no reply for a while, Penelope said a bit louder- 'Uhm, Oliver?'- she said. There was no reply from Oliver for another minute. Penelope tried again and no reply. 'Let me try.'- said Luna. 'Ayo Oliver.'- she said so loudly that it caused everyone except Oliver to look at her. Even James looked back at her momentarily. 'OLIVER!!!'- she shouted.

' Take a chill pill dude, I can hear you, I am not deaf. If you can just stop shouting 'Oliver' in my ear, I can reply to what you are saying. What should I reply to 'Oliver' huh?'- he said with a hint of mischievousness in his voice. Then he mimed Penelope and Luna shouting his name and Jacob patted him on the back, as though giving him some award after winning a contest.

Ignoring Oliver, James said 'What do you want to tell?'

'Thank God, at least someone in this car is sensible.'- Luna muttered under her breath and rolled her eyes. 'Huh?! What were you saying?'- asked Oliver, angling his ears towards Luna.

Completely ignoring Oliver, she continued 'We were thinking that if we can turn around and not go-"- she said but got interrupted. 'We are going and that's final, there is no turning back.'- said James.

Oliver and Jacob sniggered. When James looked at Oliver and Jacob, they both gave him a thumbs up and Jacob mouthed 'Well played' and Oliver mouthed 'Terrific response, she was flattened.' 'I was not flattened.'- said Luna and Oliver almost immediately covered his mouth. 'We were just testing whether you could take your own decisions or you would play as a hand puppet in Oliver's and Jacob's hands.'- said Penelope.

'Ha, in your face.'- said Luna. Even Jacob was appreciating her answer.

After Penelope's answer, neither Oliver nor Jacob didn't say anything. Meanwhile, Oliver and Jacob discussed ways to annoy Lily, Luna, and Penelope but didn't seem to find any.

There was no sound except the car's engine and the whispers of Oliver and Jacob. Oliver suddenly spoke out of nowhere 'Hey, remember that time when we were on the call and were discussing where we should go for a tour.'- he said, looking at Lily, Luna, and Penelope.

They just nodded their heads and Jacob continued where Oliver had left 'You had told us that your parents would not have allowed you to come here, then how did you manage to come along?'- he asked inquisitively. 'I left a note on my bed saying I will be back in five or six days.'- said Luna. 'After pleading a lot, I convinced them.'- said Penelope, shrugging her shoulders as if very pleased with herself. 'I snuck out as my parents don't wake up till ten, and of course, I left a note.'- said Lily carelessly, like she didn't care, or even think about what might happen once she returned.

Oliver was just about to say something else when James stopped the car abruptly, and Jacob said- 'What happened James, did the car run out of fuel, or did the tire get punctured, or was it a mechanical failure, did the brake system malfunction, or did the car collide with a tree and the headlights broke, or did the car engine overheat or-

'None of that happened.'- said James flatly. 'Then what happened?'- asked Oliver.

When James said nothing for a minute, Luna stood up and said, 'We've reached.'

CHAPTER SIX

A GAME OF TRUTH OR DARE

The pictures of Villa de Vecchi looked scary enough to creep the soul out of anybody, but this... was on a whole other level.

They got out of the car and held each other's hands as if scared that long skeletal fingers would come from behind and separate them from the group. No one wants to know (or even think) about what might happen after that.

As they approached, a chill wind whispered through the trees, sending a shiver up their spines. Broken windows leered out from behind the tattered curtains, their shattered panes reflecting only darkness.

Stepping over the threshold, they were greeted by dead silence, hanging in the air like a bunch of spider webs. Gnarled vines coiled around its weather-beaten walls, clinging like skeletal fingers to its crumbling stone façade. The moon cast its pale glow upon the abandoned mansion. The shadows danced around the mansion as if waiting patiently for prey to come and get their hands on it.

The paint, once vibrant and smooth, now peeled and flaked away in patches, revealing the weather-beaten red bricks beneath. Like splashes of bright red blood against the pale façade.

They all enter the place together, exploring places in the weather-beaten house, not knowing what might happen next. Having a feeling whether they would ever be back home or would they never...

The first thing they did was to find a place to sleep for the night. They decided to sleep near the entrance of Villa De Vecchi.

'Guys, we forgot to bring our luggage.'- said Penelope, when they finally started to settle down.

Luna clapped her forehead and James sighed heavily.

'Are we planning to go get it or just stand here and stare at each other's faces?'- asked Jacob.

'Who is going to get the luggage?'- asked James. 'One person can't go get all the luggage by himself. He or she will have to go two to three times to get all the luggage, so two or three people can go.'- said James. 'But who all will be going?'- asked Lily.

'I will.'- said Jacob. 'Guys, I know it's a bit creepy, but if we stick together, nothing is going to happen.'- said Luna. 'So, you are saying that if we go somewhere alone, something WILL happen.'- said Penelope.

'That's not what I meant to ', started Luna but Jacob interrupted her and said, 'Will anyone else be coming, or shall I and Luna go.'- he said, completely ignoring Luna's annoyed face. 'I'll come.'- said Lily.

'Fine, so you and James stay here while we get the luggage,'-said Jacob, looking at Penelope.

With this, they went outside and immediately spotted the bright red jeep in the darkness of the night.

Jacob opened the car trunk and started to take out the luggage. When all the luggage was out, Lily spotted something in the car's trunk and asked Jacob to open the trunk. He opened the trunk.

The moment the trunk was opened, two hands grabbed the shoulders of Lily from behind and she screamed in terror.

She started to panic, trying to pull the hands off her shoulders, but they held on tightly, making Lily even more scared.

Neither Luna nor Jacob was helping her. The next moment, the grip of the hands loosened and she turned around to find Oliver and Jacob laughing loudly and Luna chuckling slightly.

'Luna, you too.'- said Lily, surprised. 'This was expected from Oliver and Jacob, but not you.'- she said, on the verge of crying. 'Hey Lily, come on, it was just a prank, don't take it seriously.'- said Luna, and hugged Lily to comfort her.

Jacob and Oliver were still laughing.

'If you guys are done laughing, can we take the luggage back inside?'- asked Lily, clearly irritated.

Oliver took his stuff almost immediately and ran towards the mansion, leaving Lily, Luna and Jacob behind.

'What has come over you Jacob?'- asked Lily. Seeing the blank and confused look at Jacob's face, she said, 'I mean, you were so much better before, but lately you have changed. You have become as mischievous as Oliver. 'I was always like this; I just never showed my true self.'- replied Jacob calmly.

'Jacob, you clearly know how crazy Oliver is.'- said Lily. 'Yeah, and we don't want another crazy guy in our group, I won't be able to handle it.'- said Luna. Jacob smiled slightly at this.

After this none of the three spoke till the time they entered the mansion and were with everyone else.

As usual, Oliver was the first one to speak up after everyone had gathered. 'I'm feeling bored, do you guys want to play something?'- he asked. 'Yeah sure.'- said James.

'Are none of you feeling sleepy after such a long ride.'- asked Penelope sleepily. 'Nah.'- said Oliver. Judging by the expressions of the others, nobody except her was feeling sleepy. She sighed and said- 'What should we play then?'- she asked and sighed sleepily.

'I have a few ideas.'- said Oliver. 'We can play, uhm... yeah, got it! So, I have a few games, which include hide and seek. We can hide in this Villa and a person seeks them.'- he started off excitedly. He looked at everyone else and nobody seemed interested.

'Okay, so, yeah... I have another idea, we can play Ouija, or we can play scavenger hunt, or a photography challenge.'- said Oliver. 'A photography challenge?'- asked James keenly. 'Yeah, so we will be needing our smartphones for that. We have to take the most spooky and eerie pictures inside the Villa. The person whose pictures are the spookiest wins.'- he said.

'Hey, Ouija is a nice idea.'- said James. 'No! It's too scary.'- said Penelope. 'We anyways can't play Ouija as we don't have the Ouija board.'- said Luna. 'Common sense people.'- she said.

Seeing that no one was interested in any of the other topics, Oliver said- 'So does anyone have any better ideas?'- he asked with a hint of annoyance in his voice.

After what seemed like a minute or so, Penelope said 'Can we just sleep?'- she asked. Luna said 'Penelope, if you want to sleep, you can, but don't force us to sleep.'- she said, clearly irritated. Penelope was just about to open her mouth to argue when Lily cast both Luna and Penelope a sharp look which shut up both of them.

After another moment of silence, James finally spoke up and said ‘I have an idea that you guys may like.’- he said. ‘I hope it does not contain any of us getting separated or splitting up.’- said Luna. ‘No, so what I was thinking is that we can play that game for long, and we- ‘

‘Get to the point.’- said Oliver. ‘Truth or dare.’- said James.

‘Yeah, that seems good enough.’- said Jacob. ‘We can play that, if everyone’s okay with that.’- he said. ‘Yeah, but before we start playing, I want all of you to promise me that the dares will be safe and will not exceed any safety measures so that everyone stays safe. The dares will not be outside the Villa.’- said Jacob.

They all nodded their heads and then all of them gathered around in a circle. ‘Okay, so does anyone have a bottle?’- asked Lily. ‘I think I have it in my bag, I’ll just go and get it.’- said James and got up to get the bottle. By now, even Penelope was wide awake and was filled with energy. Penelope, who had been feeling sleepy just a minute ago, was brimming with energy and there was not the slightest hint of sleepiness on her face.

James was back with the bottle in no time. He sat down, made himself comfortable and said ‘When the bottleneck points towards someone, that individual faces the decision of either truth or dare. Meanwhile, on the opposite side, the person gets to pose a question to the chosen participant.’- said Jacob.

With this, they started the game. James spun the bottle and the first question was asked to James by Jacob. ‘Truth or dare?’- asked Jacob. ‘Truth,’ answered James. ‘Have you ever felt the presence of something paranormal or felt something unexplained that is beyond human understanding?’- asked Jacob. ‘Yes, I have felt it once, and it was in this mansion.'- he said. 'I felt as though I saw a ghost for a minute and then it vanished.'- he continued. 'I can tell you what the ghost looked like.'- he said. 'Go ahead.'- said Jacob. 'As far as I remember, it had happened when you guys were gone to take the luggage. It was the ghost of a girl; it looked shy and sleepy. She was a tall, skinny girl with a bob cut, complete moon spectacles, sky-blue eyes, fair skinned with long fingers.'- he said. 'Oh, so you mean Penelope, huh?'- said Oliver. 'You got it right.'- replied James. Penelope rolled her eyes and Jacob spun the bottle.

The next question was asked to Penelope by Oliver 'Truth or Dare?'- he asked. 'Dare.'- said Penelope, almost immediately, as if waiting for the opportunity to come from a long time.

Oliver said 'Go in that room upstairs with your phone's flashlight on. Alone, and stay there for five minutes,'- said Oliver. 'And if you don't, you have to do an even scarier dare at the end of the game.'-said Oliver.

She hesitated for a while as if she wanted to say something else but couldn't.

She went upstairs steadily and slowly; she was looking scared and freaked out but she didn't give up. Her phone's flashlight was switched on and she now disappeared out of view.

Oliver had put a timer on his phone for five minutes which he had already started.

Two minutes had passed and there was no sound in the whole mansion. 'She is doing good enough for a scaredy cat.'- said Oliver, after three minutes or so of silence. 'Do you think she would be fine.'- asked Luna, concerned about Penelope. 'Do you think she must have fainted?'- asked Lily. 'No, the fear must have kept her from fainting.'- said James thoughtfully. '

Four minutes passed, when they heard a scream from Penelope from upstairs and the next moment, Penelope was running downstairs, her face pale with fear. Looking at her pale face, Oliver sniggered but Jacob pinched him and kept him from laughing out loud.

Lily and Luna rushed to comfort Penelope. She was shivering uncontrollably, both from fear and cold. Jacob rushed and got a shawl from Penelope's bag and gave it to her.

Lily wrapped the shawl around Penelope and she and Luna made her sit between them, to keep her warm and cozy. They all paused for a while and then started the game again.

Oliver spun the bottle and Luna asked the next question to Lily. 'Truth or Dare?'- she asked. 'Truth.'- replied Lily. 'Have you ever sensed a presence or felt watched while exploring Villa de Vecchi? Describe your experience.'- asked Luna. 'Yes, I had felt a bit spooked out when I saw the mansion. There was honestly no sound except the swaying of trees, the sound of the crickets, and the sound of our footsteps. When we were outside the mansion, I looked at the windows, although there was no one in the house, I felt as if I were being watched, I had the same feeling when we entered the mansion. I have the same feeling now as well.'- answered Lily. 'Ooh, creepy.'- added James.

With this, Luna spun the bottle and the next question was asked to James by Lily.

'Truth or Dare?'- asked Lily. 'Dare.'- replied James. 'Walk alone in the dark corridors of Villa De Vecchi without any kind of light for five minutes.'- said Lily. 'Challenge accepted.'- said James, determined.

Luna set a timer on her phone for five minutes and James got up to complete the task. He handed his phone to Lily and left.

Two minutes passed, no sound.

Three minutes passed, complete silence.

Four minutes passed, and the only sound coming was faint footsteps and crickets.

Five minutes had now been completed.

'James, time's up, you can now come.'- shouted Lily over the sound of the crickets. After a few seconds, James emerged from the shadows and sat down to continue the game. He looked as if nothing had happened, he looked super casual as though the dare was child's play.

Luna spun the bottle and the next question was asked to Oliver by Luna. 'Truth or Dare?'- asked Luna. 'Dare.'- he replied.

Luna thought for a while and said, 'I dare you to take a selfie in the most eerie-looking and spooky spot you can find in Villa De Vecchi.'- she said.

Oliver took his phone, got up from his seat, and took a photo beside Luna. Before she could say anything to argue, Oliver said 'You are not eerie-looking nor you look spooky, you look VERY eerie looking and spooky and just confirming, you do look like a ghost.'- he said and went back to his place too sit down. 'Can't you simply say that you are a 'scaredy cat' and can't go to dark places alone?'- she said with a mocking tone, accompanied by a display of pity on her face.

To ignore any further arguments, Lily spun the bottle and the next question had to be asked to Luna by Oliver.

'Truth or Dare?'- he asked 'Dare.'- she replied, focused and determined for whatever would come up next.

Oliver twitched the side of his mouth in a smile and said, 'Are you sure this is what you want to do, you still have the option to change.'- he said, raising one of his eyebrows as if having a trick up his sleeve.

'No, I'm not changing my choice.'- she said, prepared to do anything. The look in Oliver's eyes said that he was ready to take revenge (for a very tiny reason, or he could be taking his revenge for getting scolded by Mr. Rupert because of her).

'Fine then. I dare you to walk outside the Villa, blindfolded, alone, without anyone's guide, and walk continuously for ten minutes without stopping, and if something happens to you, you can't run or open your blindfold.'- he said with the look of revenge in his eyes and not caring about the circumstances or the fact that she may get hurt.

'You can't give her that dare Oliver, change it.'- said Lily. 'Why?!'- said Oliver annoyed. 'Remember the promise that you gave to me before we started the game.'- said Jacob. 'You can't jeopardize the safety of Luna just for the sake of a silly dare!'- exclaimed James.

'If Luna accepts the dare, she can do it. If she doesn't then she is, '- said Oliver, who was looking at Jacob, now looked right into the eyes of Luna and said, 'A scaredy cat.'- he said and the end of his mouth twitched into a smile, not a happy one but the one which was yearning for this opportunity to call her a scaredy cat.

Luna hesitated for a while but then anyway her answer was yes.

'Luna, come on, you can say no. Don't listen to him. He's dumbed and stupid'- said Penelope, still shivering a bit, but her voice was loud enough.

Luna went to her bag, took out her handkerchief, and blindfolded herself such that nothing except darkness was visible to her.

She went outside the Villa, Lily and Penelope guiding her.

'We have reached outside the Villa; we can't guide you from now on.'- said Lily. 'Good Luck.'- said Penelope and patted her gently on the back.

'You can come back now; she is not going on the borders to fight a war and no over-smartness.'- called out Oliver's voice.

They wished her good luck once again and went inside the Villa. Luna was now all alone in the dark, not knowing what may happen the very next second.

Firstly, she was very scared of the dark, and there was no noise except the crickets and the swaying of trees. Secondly, she had nyctophobia. Thirdly, she was determined to prove to Oliver that she was not a scaredy cat but she was still a bit scared. After all, being in an abandoned mansion in the night (alone), blindfolded, would creep the soul out of anyone. Fourthly and lastly, Villa De Vecchi was famous for providing misfortune to the ones associated with it.

Luna had just realized that she had her phone in her pocket. She took her phone out and said, 'Hey Siri, set a timer for ten minutes.'- she said. 'Ten minutes timer set.'- said Siri.

With this, Luna started to walk around the Villa, not knowing where she was going. She was careful not to crash against the walls of the mansion.

While she was walking, something or someone pushed her so that she fell onto the ground. She got panicked and wanted to open her blindfold but she was certain that the person who pushed her was Oliver.

She got up and continued walking casually, although she was still scared. She could hear footsteps from behind her, she didn't turn back but continued walking. Then suddenly that person came in front of her and blocked her way. She had now completely freaked out. Her heart pounded, fear dripping from head to toe, yet she refused to remove the blindfold.

Just then, she felt a vibration in her pocket. After a few seconds, a voice said 'Ten minutes timer done.'- said Siri.

The moment Siri said it, Luna removed her blindfold to find Oliver standing in front of her, just as she expected. They were not very far away from the Villa. 'Ha, in your face.'- said Luna, sticking her tongue out.

Oliver smiled but in a kind way. 'Congrats Luna.'- said Oliver sticking out his hand to shake Luna's. 'You are not a scaredy cat after all.'- he said.

Luna was surprised by Oliver's kind attitude. He was a playful and crazy guy and never appreciated anyone. Luna stared at him for a while, thinking of any method he might have to prank her, but she couldn't find any. So, she shook his hand and astonishingly, nothing happened. 'Thanks Oliver.'- she said and they started to walk towards the Villa, still astonished by the sudden change in his behavior.

They didn't talk for the rest of the time until they reached the Villa, back with the gang of friends.

Just when Luna was about to spin the bottle, James interrupted and said 'Guys, last question as it is already twelve and we will need to leave early tomorrow to reach on time to our homes in time.'- he said. 'Right Jacob?'- he asked and looked towards him. 'Nope, nobody will sleep tonight, what have I brought so much food for? Of course, we will stay up all night and have fun.'- said Jacob enthusiastically.

'Yes, and eat a lot!'- exclaimed Oliver, brimming with energy despite the late hour.

'Uhm... Guys, it's so late, I think we should wrap up the game.'- said Lily. 'Yeah, she's right. Last question and then we'll wrap up the game.'- said Luna.

Lily spun the bottle and the last question was asked to Jacob by Oliver.

'Truth or Dare?'- asked Oliver. 'Truth.'- answered Jacob almost immediately. 'Okay, are you willing to eliminate someone present in this room.'- he asked, pretending to be serious.

'Yes.'- answered Jacob, the expression on his face changing suddenly. The chill look and the smile on his face turned into pure evil. His murderous eyes look right into Oliver's. It looked like Jacob could see Oliver's soul.

On hearing the answer, a shiver ran down Oliver's spine, but he kept on interrogating him.

'As your answer is yes, who is it?'- asked Oliver. 'I am planning to kill all of you tonight, in this very mansion. Each one of you, one by one.'- said Jacob, no change of expression on his face.

'Uhm... Guys, I think we should wrap up the game.'- said Luna loudly and boldly, breaking the eye contact of Jacob and Oliver.

When they started to wind up the game, a chill wind blew from the door and sent a cold shiver up everyone's spine except Jacob, the murderous look not leaving his eyes.

CHAPTER SEVEN

THE SUSPICIONS ARISE

The shadows started to dance on the trees, swinging from one tree to the other. It was starting to get cold and they didn't have any warm clothing, hence they decided to shift from the current place and go somewhere else.

'Seems like a good idea James.'- said Luna. 'I hope it's fine for everyone.'- asked James. Lily and Penelope nodded. 'Yeah, that seems good enough.'- said Oliver. 'And you Jacob, is it okay for you.'- asked Penelope, who had now stopped shivering completely.

Jacob looked at Penelope with the same murderous eyes and tilted his head towards her as though a madman with a creepy smile.

'Why are you acting like this Jacob?'- asked Lily. 'You are scaring me.'- said Penelope. 'Yeah, she's right. Please stop acting like this, it honestly looks like you can see my soul.'- said Luna. 'You are giving me shivers every now and then.'- said Oliver. 'You'll most probably give me nightmares.'- said James. 'Yes, it's kind of scary in this atmosphere.'- agreed Oliver.

'Okay fine, I was just having fun. I am happy you guys got scared. At least I can say that my acting is good.'- said Jacob.

Oliver sighed lightly and mouthed 'Thank God.'

With this, they started to find a warm place to rest for the night.

Luna caught up with Oliver and said 'Hey, you were the one who tried scaring me while I was doing my dare.'- she asked. 'Yeah, why?'- he asked flatly, hardly paying any attention to what she was saying.

'Uhm... actually, your behavior after that was quiet odd.'- she said. 'Odd?'- asked Oliver, now paying some attention to her.

'The mischievousness that you usually have in your eyes was not there at the moment, and you actually seemed to look more sensible. That was sweet of you.'- she said. 'Oh... yeah... uhm... Thanks Luna. No one actually appreciated me before.'- said Oliver, looking down at her as he was a bit taller than Luna.

'That was surely very nice of you but I still like you better when you are a bit crazy.'- said Luna. 'This side of you is nice, but I hope you don't lose the other one.'- she said.

'Yeah. But deep down, I'm still that old me. I'm trying to change myself; you know. Trying to find who I really am.'- he said, looking down at his bare hands.

Luna was about to say something when Lily called out to her and Luna said, 'Oliver, just a minute. And why don't you join us? Come on.'- she said and hurried off near Lily.

They all were walking in a group, talking and chit-chatting, except Oliver, who was walking behind everyone, lost in his own world.

Luna spotted that Oliver far behind everyone. She noticed that Oliver was staring right at James, and he was looking nowhere else.

Luna nudged James lightly with her elbow and said 'Ayo James, Oliver is staring at you, did you guys have a fight or something?'- she asked, voices of the other people overlapping hers. 'No.'- he replied.

James looked back at Oliver and winked. Then continued to talk with the others.

Luna went back to talk to Oliver. 'Oliver, what's wrong, why are you staring at James like that?'- she asked inquisitively.

Oliver leaned close to her as though he didn't want anyone else to hear what he was saying. 'Look at James's pocket, you will understand why I am staring at James. After you spot it, tell me how you feel.'- said Oliver, his voice barely louder than a whisper.

Luna could not understand whether Oliver was joking, whether he was actually serious, or was this just one of his silly pranks.

Without thinking, Luna looked at James's back pocket and, as though her heart had stopped beating, her brain had stopped functioning. It was as though her whole body had gone numb. It was as though her breathing had stopped. She froze in her tracks.

There it was, in James's pocket. A pistol and a pocket knife. She felt as though she wanted to run away. She wanted to warn the others but she didn't know what to do. She felt that her brain was in the place of her heart. She couldn't think.

All she could say was 'Oh no.'

She stopped, trying to calm herself down, thinking what she could do to save her friends.

'What should we do Oliver.'- she asked worryingly. 'Even I'm trying to think it through but I'm not able to find the answer.'- he said.

'We can't do anything right now, but we must first warn the others without alerting James.'- said Oliver, his mischievous side now completely vanishing, his smart and sensible side taking over.

'Yes, you are right, but do you have any ideas?'- asked Luna.

They both walked in silence for a while when suddenly Luna spoke 'We can message the others about it. Not in the group, but personally.'- she said thoughtfully.

Oliver clapped his forehead and muttered, 'Why hadn't I thought of this before?'

'I only have Penelope's and Lily's number.'- said Luna. 'And I have Jacob's.'- said Oliver.

'But won't Jacob think that it is one of your pranks?'- said Luna. 'Oh right, and we can't afford Jacob telling James that we have noticed a gun in his pocket.'- said Oliver.

'Okay then, I'll message him. Just if you're wondering how I will get his number, I can get it from the group.'- she said. 'And hurry please.'- pleaded Oliver.

Luna took out her phone and messaged everyone in a matter of a few minutes.

Everybody except James looked at their phones and then back at Luna. Luna nodded and everyone made an excuse to stop and look at James's pocket.

Jacob, made and excuse to tie his shoe's laces.

Penelope made an excuse which said that Oliver and Luna were calling her.

Lily made an excuse which said that there was a mosquito on his back which she killed.

Luna pondered why James hadn't yet realized or questioned the fact that we must have noticed the pocket knife and the pistol in his pocket.

'Hey guys, I think this looks like a comfortable place to stop for the night.'- said James cheerfully.

Jacob nodded his head and gestured everyone to sit down and relax.

'Hey, I'm feeling kind of sleepy guys, I think I'll rest for a while. You guys can continue to have fun.'- said James.

'Yeah, it's absolutely fine.'- said Jacob. 'You can sleep peacefully; we will not trouble you.'- said Lily. 'Good night.'- said Oliver. 'Sweet dreams.'- said Luna. 'And sleep quickly please.'- said Penelope.

They said this all at once and together, so none of them was understandable.

'Uhm... Thanks guys.'- said James, although he hadn't understood what they had said and sat down. He then put his head on the wall and in no time, he was asleep.

'What now?'- said Penelope. Everybody sighed and started putting their unused brains to some use.

CHAPTER EIGHT

THE UNEXPECTED

After a few seconds, Jacob said, 'I think we should run.'- he said thoughtfully. Everyone looked at him as though he was the last person to realize it. 'Of course, we should run!'- exclaimed Oliver. 'SHUSH!!!'- shushed everyone. 'Sorry.'- he said softly, realizing that he was too loud.

'If we should run, are we not?'- asked Jacob. 'Because, if we run, James can attack us. We can't run in such a big group, he will notice it and he has a pistol, remember? We don't know if he's asleep or just faking it.'- said Luna, making the last line even softer. 'We have to take the chances.'- said Oliver. 'Yeah, it's a Do or Die situation.'- said Lily. 'Oliver's right, we have to take the chances, or it will be too late.'- said Luna. 'Can we stop talking and work for once?'- said Jacob.

'Shall we stick together or shall we make groups of two?'- asked Lily. 'I think if we separate, it will be better as if one of the groups is... Uhm... you know... down, the other groups have a chance to make out safely.'- said Lily, and by down, she meant dead.

'What if the non-drivers survive?'- asked Jacob. 'That'll not happen, as each group will have a driver.'- said Oliver. 'Without wasting any time, can we decide the groups?'- asked Jacob. 'Yeah, I think I have it in mind.'- said Lily. 'So, the groups are- Penelope and Jacob, Luna and Oliver, and I will go alone. The plan is that we go in different directions so that James goes behind one, and the other escapes safely. '-she said, as she was the only one with the guts to go alone. Everybody agreed to it and there was no disagreement so they decided to proceed.

'But what if you survive? You don't even know how to drive.'- said Jacob. 'Ahh, I know how to drive, but I didn't feel like telling you guys that I can drive.' -said Lily jokingly, despite the serious atmosphere. Luna was about to say something when Lily shook her head and mouthed, 'It's Okay.'

'Come on then, what are we waiting for?'- asked Jacob and they all scurried off in different directions.

When Lily was some twenty to thirty yards away from James, she heard faint footsteps. She didn't even know how she could hear them from so far away. The footsteps were getting closer and she wasn't even very far away from the mansion.

She quickly hid behind a tree and looked out for anyone who might be visible to her, and sure enough, she could see James's blurry figure in front of her. She could make out it was James, although he was very far away from her.

Then suddenly, a hand gripped her mouth from behind. A rag was clamped over her mouth. She was struggling to release free from the strong grip of the person. She couldn't even defend herself (as she was in a very uncomfortable position) or even shout for help. She was helpless.

She was confused, James was standing right in front of her, then who was this new person?

Then, she understood it. James had been framed by someone. They had misunderstood James. Her friends were in trouble. She had to tell them, but how? The person who framed James was one of them, but who could it possibly be?

The grip of the person was very strong and tight, so it had to be a male. Oliver, or Jacob. But why would it be one of them? She tried to look up but it was too dark for anything to be visible.

Then, she smelled it. The rag which was clamped over her mouth, smelled strongly of petrol fumes. She felt as though she was about to faint. There was something on the rag. It was chloroform.

She felt as though her brain had stopped functioning, her breathing had been stopped forcefully, her heart had stopped beating, and her whole body had started to go numb. Her eyelids were now shut; she had now unwillingly fainted.

Jacob and Penelope were still running from James. 'Do you have the car keys with you?'- asked Penelope. 'Yeah, why?'- questioned Jacob. 'Just asking. If we have to leave, you know?'- she said sweetly.

Jacob didn't answer it but asked her to keep an eye out for any signs of James.

Then they suddenly heard the sounds of running footsteps. 'Penelope, come on, let's hide there.'- said Jacob, and rushed towards a corner and hid there in the dark. 'Now, Penelope you will stay here and don't move. Got me?'- he asked, still keeping an eye out for James.

After no reply for a while, Jacob said again 'Got it Penelope?'- he asked, looking back for Penelope. She was not there. Penelope didn't talk much, so it's almost like she's not even there.

He had been so busy looking out for James, that he had forgotten to keep a watch on Penelope. James must have taken Penelope while he was looking out for him. Jacob had never blamed himself more before.

Then he did the stupidest thing a person would ever do. He got up from his hiding spot, visible to James, or the person who framed him. Then, a rag clamped his mouth from the back.

The grip of the person itself was so tight that he found it hard to breathe. He had already weakened himself, holding himself responsible for Penelope's death. He could not bear to see (or feel) anything more heartbreaking than losing a friend.

The rag smelled like petrol fumes. His eyes had started to tear up. He had now totally given up. 'Penelope must have struggled with James's grip,' he thought.

He smelt the chemical in the rag once more and must have realized that he had started to faint. He hit James with his elbow but that didn't loosen the grip, or he thought it was James.

He couldn't feel his surroundings. He couldn't feel himself. Darkness had won over light and he had fainted...

On the other hand, Oliver and Luna were outside the Villa, near the car, waiting for Jacob, Penelope, and Lily to come. But little did they know, they were never going to come.

It had been almost ten minutes they had been waiting for them to come. It was three in the morning.

'They shouldn't be taking so much time to come, unless...'- said Luna and started to tear up.

She sat on her knees; her face buried in her hands, weeping softly and silently. 'Oliver, d-do yo-you think tha-that they would be s-safe?'- she murmured, her face red after crying. 'I can make no promises.'- said Oliver, as he didn't understand what else to say.

A silent tear trickled down Luna's left cheek. 'S-should we check?'- she asked hopefully.

'It would be very risky to find them. We can't risk our lives for the others.'- he said. Before Luna could argue, he said 'Before we leaved, Jacob told me to go if he didn't come, and not wait for him.'- said Oliver.

'OLIVER!!!'- shouted Luna. 'Behind you!'- she exclaimed and pointed towards something behind him.

Oliver turned back, ready to attack or dodge any punches or kicks. He didn't see anyone. He wanted to turn behind and ask Luna where James was. He didn't know how he knew it was James, he just knew.

Just then, a rag clamped over his mouth. He didn't even try to defend himself. But he tried to take a look of the person's face as he was sure that James was the same height as him, but this person was shorter than him.

As he smelled the rag, he realized that it was chloroform. He tried to hold his breath, but he soon had to release it. He had understood that the rag was clamped over his mouth by James or Jacob. But why would Jacob do that? It had to be James.

Just before loosing his senses, a thought popped up in his mind, 'Where was Luna?'

It would be good if Luna ran away at the right moment.

Oliver was thinking so rapidly that he didn't even realize that he had fainted.

***

The next moment, he found his mouth and eyes, taped up. Hands and legs, tied up in a knot which would not come out.

He heard some muffling noises, which he assumed to be his friends.

He tried to untie the knot, when a voice spoke up, 'Oliver, don't be silly, you won't be able to untie the knot. I'm a professional dude, what do you expect? And Guys, I hope you are comfortable, because you are not escaping this place until I want you to. Yeah, and I'm starting to feel relly bored now.'- said the unfamiliar voice. It seemed of a girl.

'Hey Jacob, remeber you told me that 'what's fun without a little danger, right?'- said the unfamiliar voice. 'Yeah, and you also said that what's fun without that feeling in which your heartbeat increases and you know it's dangerous but you anyways do it.'- she said

They knew every single voice. The voice was neither Luna's, nor Lily's or Penelope. Then who was this new person?

'Do you wanna play a game?'- asked the unfamiliar female voice. She cleared her throat and said- 'So the game- ', started the female voice, but was interrupted by strange banging and struggling noises beside Lily.

'Aww, Luna, what is it now?'- asked the unfamiliar female voice. There were some more muffling noises and the voice said, 'Ah, sorry Luna.'- she said and the sound of heels was echoing through the room.

Lily felt the cloth of the female's dress on her hand, and it was cotton, pure cotton and there was only one person wearing cotton that night in their group.

'Who are you, why are you here?'-asked Luna boldly. 'Why are you doing this? What have we done to you?'-

said Luna, her voice now cracking up. In a few seconds, everybody heard the soft cries of Luna.

The cry of Luna was so heartbreaking that Lily, Jacob, and Oliver felt a tear fall down their cheek.

'I've got a bad feeling about you.'-said the voice in a sing-song way and put the tape back on Luna's mouth.

Then they heard the echoing of heels and the familiar voice spoke 'You want to know who I am? Then listen.'- said the voice bitterly.

'I'll tell you who I am.'- said the unfamiliar female in the sweet, kind, soft voice of Penelope.

Two Days Later

WANTED IN ROMA

Five seventeen-year-olds attempt to murder

Six school-going teenagers go to explore Villa De Vecchi in search of adventure. All six friends were having fun when five friends attacked a girl from their gang.

The girl's name is Penelope.

The girl had made out safely, although there was no trace of the five young adults. Penelope Stirling had come to the police station at six in the morning.

The girl had significant injuries on her knees, head, and face. She is currently under medical observation.

When asked about her parents, Ms. Stirling said that she didn't have any and was thus an orphan.

As for the teenagers, here are the names.

Luna Lockwood

Oliver Holloway

Lily M. Whitlock

Jacob Everhart

James Ravenscroft

If you know them, kindly contact us at http://www.wantedinrome.com

www.ingramcontent.com/pod-product-compliance
Lightning Source LLC
LaVergne TN
LVHW040914150826
845672LV00007B/2041

* 9 7 9 8 8 9 3 2 2 5 9 0 7 *